# Kids vs. Nature

## Book 4

# Surviving Cougar Mountain

Illustrated by:
Mary Mon~~ette~~ G. Barbaso

W
K

D1304381

ISBN: 978-1-63578-012-3

Contact information for Libro Studio LLC can be found at www.LibroStudioLLC.com

# Chapter 1

*– Sorry, this story is longer than the others.*
*Trust me, I wish it wasn't.*

Something small and white hit the back of Tyler's head. It was obvious who threw it. John was already tearing another corner off his worksheet and crumpling it into a tiny little ball.

"Knock it off," Tyler said.

"What?" John asked, with a fake tone of innocence.

"You know what."

"I didn't do anything," John said. "Now stop bothering me. I'm trying to work here."

John picked up his pencil and pretended to work on the bell work problems. Other kids saw he was joking and chuckled. Even Mark laughed.

Tyler glared at John, then returned to his work. John waited, then slowly crept down the aisle and picked up the binder Tyler kept under his chair.

John sat down. He paged through one of Tyler's notebooks. "What are these," he muttered.

I glanced at the notebook. The pages were covered with drawings. I saw sketches of a moose sticking its head in the water. And a raccoon holding a sock in its mouth.

"It must be his mom," John whispered. "She's a cow just like him."

Others giggled some more. John seemed to enjoy their attention.

John hid the binder under a pile of his own papers. A few minutes later Tyler leaned to the side and reached under his chair. He sat up quickly. "Hey, where'd you put it?" Tyler asked.

John shrugged. "Put what?"

"My binder, I know it was you," Tyler said.

"Have you guys seen a binder?" John asked. No one answered, except for a few who shook their heads. "See, we don't have it."

Tyler looked at me. I glanced away. I didn't want to get involved. Not if it had anything to do with John Marten.

Tyler's eyes scanned the room for his binder. Eventually he turned and continued working. Just then, the pulse of light came. The whole room became bright and I had to close my eyes.

# Chapter 2
# Pine Trees

When I opened my eyes, we were in a circle again, wearing our jeans, t-shirts, and leather shoes too.

Pine trees were all around us. Above the tree tops were rocky mountain peaks. I could tell we were on a slope of a mountain, because the ground was higher in one direction and lower in the other.

We leaned over the screen as Katie opened the mission page.

It read, "Shoot the king of the mountain."

"Get it?" Melisa asked. Regular lions are the king of the jungle, so a mountain lion is the king of the mountain."

Katie put her phone away. "Yea we're not stupid," she said.

"Hey, we should read about them first," Tyler said.

Katie took the phone back out and typed 'mountain lion' in The Firefly Mission's search bar.

"It says they can climb trees and sometimes hide on the branches," Tyler said.

Katie looked at the branches directly above us. "I have a bad feeling about this," she said. "A moose was dangerous enough. This thing has claws and teeth."

I pointed to the section that talked about size. "And they can weigh over 200 pounds," I added.

Melisa looked at me. Her eyebrows narrowed. "Okay, that's not helping."

"They're probably more afraid of us that we are of them, right?" Tyler asked.

"Speak for yourself," Katie said.

Melisa picked up the backpack and canteens. "Hey, looks like we get more supplies this time."

In the other missions the backpack was limp and saggy looking. This time it was bulging, and blue fabric stuck out of the opening.

Melisa picked up the bag and bounced it up and down. "It's really light."

"See what's in it," Katie said.

Melisa pulled some of the blue fabric out. "A coat," she said.

Melisa raised a jacket. It looked like a sweatshirt, but the way the fabric moved made it clear that it was thicker and more insulated than a normal sweatshirt.

"Stupid app," Katie said. "Doesn't it know it's like eighty degrees out here?"

"Hey, anything's better than nothing," Melisa said. She pulled three more jackets, the pot, matches, knife, and ropes from the backpack. Then she unfolded the top of the bag against itself over and over again. "I've got something to show you guys. I was doing more research and saw a picture of a bag that looked just like this one. They're water proof."

Melisa bent the folded area far enough for the two side clips to meet. The buckle clicked into place. "See," she said. "Now water can't get inside. Even if it rains or if you guys tip another canoe, our matches won't get wet."

"Sweet," Tyler said. He looked at the backpack with admiration. He felt how tight the folded area was kept in place by the clip, then put the bag onto his shoulders.

# Chapter 3
# Tough Going

It seemed like we hiked for hours, probably because it was hours, but we didn't get far. There were too many fallen trees in the way. It was hard walking around them and climbing over their tops. The only thing going in our favor was that we decided to walk downhill. After our desert mission, no one was in the mood to do any more climbing.

"Let's take a rest," Tyler said.

Beads of sweat dotted his forehead. His shirt was damp.

"Sounds good," I said, because I felt warm too.

Melisa and Tyler sat on a dead tree.

Katie was about to sit next to them when she said, "Do you guys hear that?"

All I could hear was a light breeze making the trees sway.

"It sounds like water," Katie said, after no one answered.

Instead of continuing downhill, Katie walked sideways along the mountain.

We had just stopped. I didn't feel like moving again, but Katie kept walking.

"Well, I could use some water," Tyler said.

He followed Katie through the forest. Me and Melisa finally fallowed too.

It didn't take long before I started to hear a "Sshhing," sound. A while later, it was a quiet rumble. The rumble grew louder and louder. Eventually the forest thinned out, allowing us to see the fast-moving stream that was making the noise. Now that we were out of the trees we could see a bluish-green lake where our mountain met the bottom of another mountain.

"I say we follow the stream to the lake," Melisa said. "We can look for tracks along the way. The mountain lions probably rely on both to get water."

Katie climbed onto the rocks beside the stream. She lowered herself onto her hands and knees and reached for the water with her canteen.

"Careful," Melisa said. "if you fall, you'll get swept away."

Katie ignored Melisa's warning and held her canteen in the water. She screwed the cover back on and held it out for me to take. "Hand me yours and I'll fill them up for you," she said to us.

Katie filled our canteens. When Tyler got his back, he opened it and lifted it to his mouth.

"Stop," I said. "We need to purify it first."

"But it's clean," Tyler said. "It's not like its muddy desert water or the swamp water like last time."

"I know the water looks clear, but you still need to purify it," I told him.

"There could be bacteria or parasites in there," Melisa added.

Tyler screwed the cover back on, then sat on a rock. I gathered dead pine needles and twigs, while Melisa dug the matches out of the backpack.

Melisa smiled at me when I brought the kindling to her. "You did some research," she said.

I nodded.

"Thanks," she said. "You might have saved his life."

# Chapter 4
# Sweet Treats

All the rocks and trees still made it difficult to walk down the mountain. We didn't find any tracks either. Most of the stream's edges were covered with rocks and boulders, making it hard for animals to leave footprints. The sun sank below the far peak, leaving us in the mountain's giant shadow. We found a place to camp and agreed to keep walking to the lake the next day.

"I'm starving," Tyler said, when we woke up.

My stomach had been growling all night too. When I was younger my mom sent me to bed without supper a few times, but this was worse because we hadn't been able to eat a lunch either. Even the school's nasty tuna casserole would have been nice.

"We can make a fish trap when we get to the lake," Melisa said. "I think it'll be hard to make one in the stream."

"What's that?" Tyler asked.

Melisa shook her head. "I'll show you when we get there."

After refilling our canteens and purifying them, we resumed our hike. My legs were sore, especially the muscles connecting to my knees. They were worked the hardest while walking downhill.

"Can we eat these?" Tyler asked, a few hours into our hike.

He was leaning over a short bush that had berries dangling from its branches.

"Are those blue berries," I asked, since the berries were a purplish-black color.

"I don't know," Tyler said. He picked a few. "They look a little different, don't they?"

Katie took a picture of them.

"Analyzing Image..." the app said. "Huckleberry."

"Pretty sure those are edible," Melisa said.

Katie read through the information on huckleberries before nodding. "Yup, they are."

Katie was the first to taste one. The rest of us were quick to follow.

The berries were good, and I'm not just saying that because we were starving. They looked a lot like blueberries but were even sweeter tasting.

At first there weren't that many berry bushes, but as we walked away from the stream, we found more. The bushes deeper in the forest grew taller too. The ones by the stream were about three feet tall. The ones inside the forest were so tall I couldn't reach the berries on the top branches. They were probably nine or ten feet high.

Eventually we found a different berry, that the app called a thimbleberry. It was a dark red color and looked like a raspberry to me. They had a stronger taste. The best way I can describe it is that it was spicy and tart at the same time, but in a good way. The only bad thing was that the thimble berries were really soft, so a lot of times they squished when picking them. Their juices got on our hands and stained them a pinkish-red color.

After our stomachs were full, we picked enough berries to fill the cooking pot. Then we took the jackets out of the backpack and tied them around our waist. That way we had room to fill the bottom of the backpack with berries too.

# Chapter 5
# Setting the Trap

It was late afternoon by the time we made it to the lake. We looked for tracks along the shoreline, but not very long. There were still too many rocks and not enough sand to find many tracks.

We decided to camp where the stream entered the lake. Me and Tyler helped Melisa carry large rocks into the water, so we could build a fish trap. We wore our shoes in the water, because the lake's rocky bottom would've hurt our feet without them. Melisa was smart enough to at least take her socks off first. I didn't think of doing that.

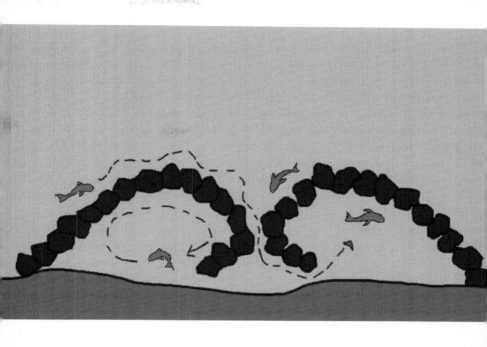

The lake was so cold, it felt like it was refrigerated. That's why Katie didn't help build the trap. The skin on my feet and legs quickly began to sting and turn red, so we worked as fast as we could, sloppily splashing and dropping rocks here and there.

"See, now during the night, when the fish swim along the shoreline looking for food, they'll think the rocks are the shore and swim right into the trap," Melisa explained. "Since the opening is so small, they won't be able to find their way back out again. They'll swim in circles."

"Move that one over more," Katie told me as I dropped another rock in the water. "You're making it lop sided."

I wanted to tell her to get in the water and do it herself, but I didn't. Eventually we finished the trap, squeezed as much water out of our socks and shoes as possible and put them next to the fire to dry. We laid on the ground and held our feet by the flames. My feet had blisters, from all the walking the past two days. It looked like Melisa and Tyler's feet had some too.

For supper, we ate from our supply of huckleberries and thimbleberries. They still tasted as good as ever, but I could really have gone for a cheeseburger and French fries instead.

"Your shoe's on fire," Katie said.

I looked down to where I had left my shoes to dry. Smoke was rising from the front of one. I grabbed the heel and flung it away from the flames. I picked it back up after it stopped smoking. There was a hole, with singed edges where the big toe is supposed to go.

"Shoot," I said.

"Don't put it so close to the fire next time," Katie said.

I felt the inside of the shoe. It was still wet. The outside must have dried off a lot quicker. Apparently, it got a little too hot.

# Chapter 6
# Jacket Weather

The air was colder the second night. Sleeping by the fire wasn't enough to keep warm. Part way through the night I put my jacket on. This helped a lot. The fabric was surprisingly warm, but not warm enough. Eventually it got so cold I was even shivering with the jacket on. The parts of my body facing the fire felt alright, but the other parts felt like they were freezing. I was cold, and tired, and uncomfortable for what seemed like hours. I must have eventually fallen back to sleep, because the next thing I knew it was bright outside again.

Katie held her arms close to her body. Sometime during the night, she had put her jacket on too. "That was miserable," she said, her breaths forming wisps of condensation as she spoke.

Dirt and pine needles near the fire looked the same as they had the day before, but further away from the heat, a thin layer of frost covered the ground. Tree branches were frosted too. The lake also looked different, because there was mist rising from the water's surface.

"Let's start looking for a mountain lion already," Katie said. "I don't want to spend another night here."

Melisa was the first to venture away from the fire. She walked to the fish trap and peered in the water.

"Nothing," she said.

Tyler came beside her and looked in the water too. "Maybe we made it wrong,"

"No, we made it right. It probably just doesn't work quite as well as the internet made it sound," Melisa said.

"We won't have to worry about fish if we finish the mission," Katie said. "Let's look for tracks."

We walked around the lake. My muscles and joints were sore at first, but the longer we walked the less I noticed. It was the blisters on my feet that felt worse. They stung every time I took a step.

Like I said earlier, most of the shoreline was also rocky, so it was hard to find tracks, but there were a few areas of sand and mud. They had raccoon tracks for sure. Melisa thought the ones that looked like little dog tracks were from a fox. We figured the ones that looked like small moose tracks were deer. There were a few other kinds of small tracks there too, but we didn't have any good guesses for what they were.

"Wait a minute," Melisa said. She stopped and looked across the lake. "We can't just walk around the lake and get back to our campsite."

"Why not?" I asked.

"We camped next to the stream. If we keep going this way, we'll have to cross it to get back."

I pictured the stream in my mind. As far as streams go, it wasn't huge, but we would need to swim a ways to get to the other side.

"She's right," I said. "I'm not swimming. It was cold enough making the fish trap."

Katie's shoulders slumped as she looked further down the shoreline to where the stream was. By this time, we had already walked three fourths of the way around the lake. "Why couldn't you think of that earlier?" she said.

Melisa put her hands on her hips. "At least I thought of it. You would've walked all the way there before figuring it out."

We didn't say anything else. I think we were all kind of crabby and upset with needing to hike even further to get back to camp than we had planned.

"I think I found one," Tyler said, when we were halfway back. He ran ahead of us and crouched next to a set of tracks. Even from a distance, I could tell they were big tracks.

"Those aren't cougar tracks," Katie said. She tapped the screen on her phone a few times, until she came to the information page about mountain lions and scrolled down to a picture of their tracks.

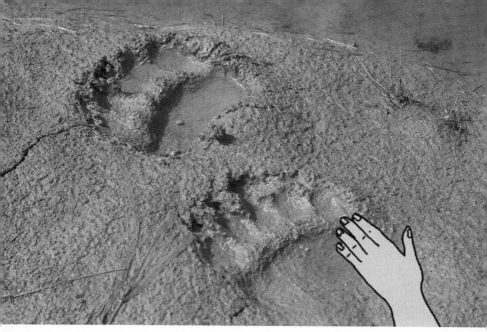

"See, they should look like big cat tracks," Katie said, and held the phone out for Tyler to see.

"So, what are these?" I asked.

We stared at the tracks, but nobody made a guess. I felt creeped out when I realized that they hadn't been there when we first walked past that part of the shoreline. We would have noticed tracks that big, and some of the paw prints were covering the shoe prints we had made. I looked into the forest to see if anything was watching us.

"They have to be bear tracks," Melisa said. "What else could be that big?"

Melisa put her hand next to the track to compare its massive size.

I think we have a match," Katie said. She turned the phone to show us a picture of grizzly bear tracks, and they looked exactly like the ones in the mud.

# Chapter 8
# Splitting Up

Nobody said that they were scared, but we stayed close to each other the rest of the way back. We walked faster too.

"We need a shelter," Melisa said, after we rebuilt the fire. "Last night was too cold to sleep in the open."

"What we need is more food," Tyler said.

He reached into the backpack and pulled out a handful of berries, and I did the same. They still tasted fine, but they had grown soft and mushy since we first picked them. I'll admit, they were better than nothing, but didn't really take our hunger away. And believe me; two days of hiking could really work up a person's appetite.

Melisa reached her hand into the backpack too. Instead of grabbing a hand full of berries, she pulled out the ropes.

"We need a shelter first," she said. "We can last days, even weeks without food, but we could freeze to death in hours without a shelter."

"But doesn't our body need energy to make heat?" Tyler asked.

"Yea, but right now that isn't as important," Melisa said.

"Can't we just split up?" I asked, since what I really wanted was food and a shelter. "Two of us can build shelters and two can look for more food."

Tyler was quick to raise his hand. "I'll look for food," he said.

"I'll go with if no one else wants to," I offered. "I found a website that showed how to build traps and deadfalls."

Melisa glanced at Katie, and then rolled her eyes. "Whatever. Just don't get lost."

"We won't," Tyler said.

"Yea, we'll make sure that we can hear the stream at all times," I said.

I tried not to smile as Tyler and I left. I was excited to build some traps. How impressive would it look if we not only found some more berries, but could actually catch a rabbit or some kind of meat to bring back for the girls too? Seriously, is there anything more manly than putting food on the table? Well, not that we had a table, but you know what I mean.

"I say we set up a couple traps, before looking for berries," I told Tyler. "That way when we finish picking we can check the traps."

Tyler nodded. "Sure."

# Chapter 9
# Deadfalls

The first thing you need to do when making a deadfall is find a good place to build one—A place where animals go frequently. We chose a spot near a rabbit trail.

Next, we had to find the right supplies. We found the stone we needed near the stream. It was large and flat, but most importantly, it was heavy. We had to each hold a side to carry it into the forest, then Tyler held it in place while I stacked the sticks in a particular way to hold it up.

Stacking the sticks was the hardest part. The trick is to stack them so that they're strong enough to hold the rock up, but sensitive enough for an animal to knock them over.

At first our sticks were too thin and snapped when Tyler leaned the stone on them. After that, we found stronger sticks, but they kept buckling out from under the stone until we modified their ends to make them fit against each other better.

We finally got the sticks to hold, with one stick poking out sideways. That sideways stick is called the trigger. You put bait for the animals underneath it, so they accidently bump the trigger when they try to get the food. When that happens, the rock should slam down and either kill the animal or pin it to the ground until you return.

We used a twig to test the deadfall a few times. Just tapping the trigger wasn't enough to make the rock fall, but with a little pressure the sticks would twist and make everything collapse.

"Perfect," I said, after setting up the trap for the last time. "Now, do you have any carrots?"

"Sorry, fresh out of carrots," Tyler said. "But rabbits like clovers, don't they?"

I nodded, and we piled clovers and grass under the trigger until it looked like we had a rabbit sized salad to entice them with.

Finally, the trap was finished, and we were able to start searching for berries.

The other day we had found most of the berries higher up the mountain. Since we didn't have time to climb that high again (and didn't want to), we decided to just look deeper in the forest. This didn't seem to help us though. We only found a few more berries.

"What about this," Tyler asked. He picked an acorn off the ground, beneath one of the few trees that actually had leaves on it. "I thought I've heard of people eating them."

I wasn't so sure. Eating acorns? If people could eat acorns why wouldn't more people do it?

Tyler set one of the acorns on a log, then used a stone to crack the shell open. We looked at the pale colored nut inside. The rock had made it fall apart, but there were still some larger chunks that Tyler put in the palm of his hand.

"Shouldn't we cook it first?" I asked.

"Yea, I think you roast them, just like other nuts," Tyler said.

My mouth watered. As hungry as I was, I think anything roasted would have sounded delicious.

The air had grown cool by the time we made it back. I was surprised to see two shelters beside the fire, one for the girls and one for us guys. The shelters were green, because the girls had broken off live pine branches and set them on the shelter, so that their needles would form a roof.

Melisa looked up at us. "It's about time," she said. "What took you so long?"

"Its hard work finding food," I explained.

"What'd you get?" Katie asked. Tyler held the backpack open for her to see. "Acorns?"

"Good thinking guys," Melisa said. "They're supposed to have a lot of nutrition."

Katie held her stomach then crawled into one of the shelters. "Seriously, are you guys trying to make me barf?"

# Chapter 10
# Bitter

It took a while to crack the acorns open, but eventually we had enough nuts to start roasting. Well, at least me and Tyler started roasting. We found large flat stones by the lake and set them near the fire. Then we set acorns on the stones and waited for them to cook.

Melisa said she had found a recipe online for acorn soup, so she put some water in the pot to try boiling the nuts. "Its cold out here," Melisa said, "We'll want some soup to warm us."

Water always takes a while to boil, so the roasted acorns finished first. They turned brown and shriveled a little, so we used a stick to push the stones away from the fire and waited for them to cool.

Tyler picked up a piece and held it under his nose. "Doesn't smell bad," he said.

He tossed a smaller piece in his mouth and chewed. At first his eyes widened. Then he scrunched his nose and spit the acorn out.

Katie covered her mouth with her hand. "Seriously? That's gross."

Tyler leaned on his knees and continued to spit a few of the smaller pieces out. "It's even grosser when it's in your mouth," he said.

"Maybe that was a bad one," I said. "Try another."

Tyler shook his head. "You try one."

Now I felt like everyone was watching me. I didn't want to look scared, so I picked up a piece. It wasn't a tiny piece, because that would make me look like a wimp. It wasn't a huge piece either. After all, I don't think I had ever seen Tyler spit food out of his mouth before, and he's the kid who ate blueberries out of his wet socks and is known for dipping his peaches in ranch dressing.

I put the acorn in my mouth and pretended to chew. It didn't seem that bad, so I put it between my teeth and bit a little. That's when I realized that Tyler wasn't kidding when he said it was gross.

As soon as the acorn crushed, a bitter taste filled my mouth. Imagine nibbling a chunk of ear wax, except ten times more bitter. I know. Gross, right? I wanted to spit it out too, but instead I continued to act tough and swallowed it.

"How was it?" Melisa asked.

"Not that great," I admitted.

I tried to keep a straight face while unscrewing the top of my canteen and taking a drink. It helped get some of the taste out of my mouth, but the bitterness still lingered.

# Chapter 11
# Chop Sticks

Melisa's acorn soup eventually boiled, and she set the pot to the side to cool.

"Who wants the first taste?" she asked, holding it toward me and Tyler.

I've heard people say that when you're truly hungry you'll eat just about anything. Well, I imagine that I could be on the verge of starving to death and I'd still struggle to eat acorns.

"Na, it's your soup. You should get the first bite," I said.

Katie smiled as Melisa stared at the pot. "I need a spoon or something," she said.

We looked around the campsite.

Katie walked to a nearby tree and snapped off long slender twigs. "Try these." Katie held them in one hand like a pair of chop sticks. She pinched them together a few times, and pretended she was using them to pick something up.

Melisa took the sticks from Katie and tried to hold them in one hand. I could tell by the way she almost dropped one that she wasn't good at using chop sticks.

"Here. Like this." Katie said. She took the sticks back from Melisa and pretended she was picking up an invisible piece of food.

"You just do it," Melisa said.

"I'm not trying it," Katie said, but dipped the sticks into the soup and pulled out one of the acorn chunks that had settled to the bottom. She bounced the sticks a few times to let the water drip off the acorn. "Here," she said. "Open up."

Melisa tilted her head back. She opened her mouth and Katie fed her like a mama bird would feed its chick. Melisa chewed the chunk. I waited for her to spit it out, throw up, or have some kind of reaction. Let's just say I was a little disappointed. She didn't even make a funny face.

"You're right. It's not that great, but it's not that bad either." Melisa said. "But I have an idea. Melisa opened the backpack and pulled out some mushy berries. "Get me another one," she said.

Katie picked up another acorn with the chop sticks and fed it to Melisa, but before Melisa chewed she put the berries in her mouth too.

"Now that's a little better," she said.

Katie put some berries in her mouth, then added an acorn. After chewing, she put a few more in her mouth and really started chowing down.

It took a while before me and Tyler worked up enough guts to try the acorns again. To our surprise the acorn pieces from the soup were a lot better than the ones we had roasted. They were still mildly bitter, but most of the intense taste was gone. Once the boiled acorns were mixed with the sweet berries, they really weren't bad.

We cracked the rest of the acorns and continued to boil and eat them, even after the sky turned dark. For the first time in a few days, my stomach didn't feel completely empty. Melisa said it's because the acorns are seeds, and seeds usually have "high fat content." I don't really know what that means. I don't understand a lot of the things that Melisa says. All I know is that I felt good after finishing the meal.

# Chapter 12
# Nothing but Mush

The next day we followed the stream back up the mountain, to replenish our supply of berries. We checked the dead fall on the way, but it was empty. That wasn't the only disappointment either. There were hardly any berries left, and the ones remaining were shriveled and mushy.

"There was frost the other morning," Melisa said. "I bet they froze out."

We collected as many mushy berries as possible, but realized our berry gathering days were probably over.

It was late afternoon by the time we made it back to the lake.

Tyler ran to the water. "Hey, you guys," he shouted.

A splash appeared from inside the fish trap. That made the rest of us rush to the lake too. Eventually I could see two fish swimming in circles. They followed the rock walls all the way around the trap, each time swimming right past the little opening where they entered.

"Hurry, help me close it up," Melisa said. She stepped into the water, picked up a stone, and dropped it in front of the trap's opening.

Tyler and I helped Melisa block the fish's only way out. Once a pile of rocks covered their exit, they were trapped for good.

Tyler was the first to step into the trap. He tried catching the fish, but they were quick, and he was not. No matter how quiet Tyler waded toward them, the fish always darted away. Finally, Tyler lunged at them. Watching him plunge below the surface made me shudder. I was only knee deep, and the water already felt freezing.

Tyler jumped at the fish a few more times, until one of them got so spooked it leaped into the air and jumped right out of the trap.

"Stop it," Melisa yelled. "You're chasing them out."

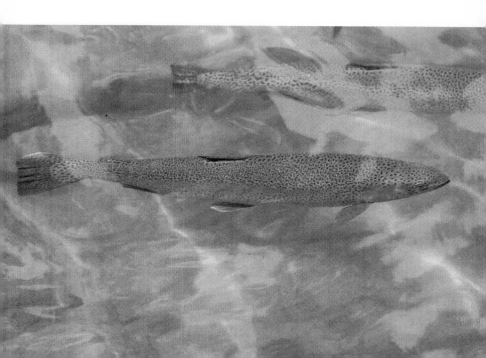

Tyler left the water. He crossed his arms and shivered on shore for a few moments, then waddled to the fire pit. His whole body looked stiff as he leaned over and blew on the old coals from the fire. Wisps of smoke appeared. He threw pine needles into the pit. Soon a flame flickered

"Come on," Melisa said. She stepped into the fish trap. "We'll need to work as a team."

I took a step deeper and to my surprise, Katie came in the lake too. Melisa waited until Katie and I were right next to her, then we slowly walked toward the fish. We put our hands in the water and spread our arms out as wide as we could, so that we could herd the fish toward the edge of the trap. The fish darted back and forth as we closed in on it.

"Let's make it to go by the shore line. That way it won't jump out like the other one," Melisa said.

We slowly forced it to swim shallower. Eventually the water was so shallow it's back poked out of the lake as it swam. It must have realized it was getting trapped, because it tried to dart past me.

I reached out and grabbed it. The fish was way too slippery though. It flopped from my hands but didn't get past me. It swam to Melisa, then tried to turn back. There wasn't enough room though. It swam right onto the shore with the front half of its body. Melisa pushed it further on land and pinned it against the ground. Katie grabbed its tail, and I came to help pull it from the water.

43

# Chapter 13
# Baked Fish

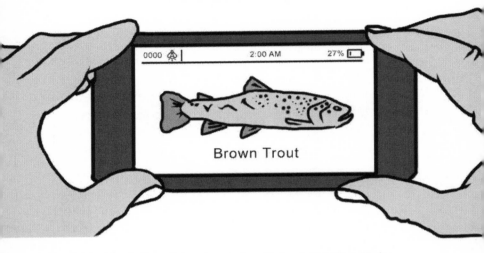

0000    2:00 AM    27%

Brown Trout

Nobody knew how to gut a fish. Luckily, Tyler volunteered to do it. It's a gross job. Let's just say it took him quite a while to wash all the slime, blood, and scales from his hands.

We had Tyler hang the fish on a stick, then took turns roasting it over the fire. Some of the edges got a little burned, but it was still tasty.

We used chopsticks again to eat. I was getting a lot better at using the sticks too. It's really not that hard if you practice long enough. The toughest part was picking all the bones out of the meat. We had to use our fingers for that.

When we finished, the tail, head, back bone, and a few ribs were left. We tossed these scraps into the fire pit

"That was delicious," Tyler said. "I wish the trap caught fish every day."

"Maybe we should build more," I said. "The more traps we have the more fish we'll catch."

"Using statistics in our favor," Melisa said. "Good idea."

We made more fish traps the rest of the evening. We stacked rocks until the water became too cold to stand. After warming up by the fire, we'd go right back to work. We built traps this way until the sun set and we had five traps made.

As you can imagine we were tired from the hiking and building. After warming up by the fire one more time, we crawled into the shelters.

"With all those traps, we better get fish every single night," Tyler said.

I nodded. "We'll probably catch so many we'll have to throw some back."

"You guys talk like we're going to be here a long time," Katie said. "Maybe we should focus more on finding a mountain lion instead."

"We haven't even found signs of a mountain lion," Melisa pointed out. "Having long-term plans is a good thing."

"But we should do more to look for them," Katie insisted. She took out her phone and read the information about mountain lions one more time. "Maybe we're looking in the wrong places."

"We can try walking around the lake again," I suggested. "It's been a while since we looked for tracks there."

Suddenly her phone made a noise I hadn't heard before. "Doo-Daa..."

"Shoot," Katie said. She tapped the phone's screen a few more times. "Shoot, shoot, shoot!"

"What's wrong," Tyler asked.

"Low batteries."

Melisa sat up strait. "You're kidding, right?"

Katie shook her head.

"What did you expect," I said. "We've been here four days now."

"Don't you get it," Melisa said. "We need the phone to bring us back."

The screen went dark as Katie held down the power button. Then she slid the phone into her jacket's pocket and zipped it shut.

# Chapter 14
# Breathing

When I woke up I thought I was in a Jurassic Park movie. You know how whenever a T-rex comes close to someone it sniffs the air with long, loud, deep breaths. Well, before I even opened my eyes, I could hear breathing that sounded kind of like that. The breaths were long, loud, and deep.

I opened my eyes a split second later and saw a bear walk out of the darkness and up to our fire pit. The flames in the fire had burned down. All that was left was a large pile of red glowing coals to keep us and the shelters warm.

I didn't know if I should yell, or run, or what I should do. I could hardly believe what I was seeing. The bear smelled the fire then stuck its nose next to the coals. I could see its mouth moving and could hear its lips smacking together as it nibbled at the fish bones lying in the fire pit.

I nudged Tyler, who was sleeping just a few feet away from me.

"What?" he asked.

"We gotta go," I whispered. "Bear."

Tyler's eyes widened when he saw the bear and he instinctively stood up.

A lot of people think they understand that bears are big animals, but until you see one up close, you have no idea just how big they are. The bear was on all four feet while it was eating out of the fire pit, and Tyler wasn't that much taller than the bear's shoulder.

The bear seemed irritated that Tyler had moved. It stood on its hind legs and peered down at Tyler and me, then snorted a few times.

The snorting must have woken Katie, because she screamed. The bear dropped back down to all fours and spun to look at her. Now that the bear was distracted I got up and tried to run out of the shelter. The bear spun back in my direction and swatted me with its paw. It didn't get me with a direct hit, but it was enough to knock me off my feet and send me flying a few yards.

From the ground, I could see the others had left the shelters and were scrambling into the forest. The bear lunged toward me but came to a stop a few feet away. It backed up a couple steps then used its front feet to swat dirt into the air. It snorted and slowly backed up to the fire pit.

I stayed as still as possible, until I could hear it eating again. Then I slowly stood.

The bear changed its position a little, but never lifted its head from the pit. That's when I made a run for it too.

# Chapter 15
# Are We All Here?

I ran through the forest and didn't stop. I wanted to get as much distance between me and that bear as possible. Branches hit my face. I stumbled over roots and rocks. It was too dark to really know where I was going. Finally, I heard Melisa talking.

"It's coming," she said, as I ran toward the sound of her voice.

"It's me," I said.

"Where is it?" she asked.

"I think it's still at camp. Where are you guys?"

"This way. Keep coming," Tyler said.

I found them high in a tree. All I could see was their dark figures sitting on two separate branches.

"Get up here," Melisa urged.

I climbed and found an empty branch to sit on.

"Higher," Melisa said. "It'll still reach you there."

I stepped on Tyler's branch and pulled my way up to a place in the tree even higher than he was. "Where's Katie?" I asked.

Melisa didn't shake her head much, but it was enough to make her tree branch shake too. "She ran the other way."

"How long do we have to stay up here?" Tyler asked.

I could tell by the way he readjusted himself on the branch that his butt was already sore and uncomfortable.

"I'm staying up here all night if I can," Melisa said.

That was my intention too. I had no desire to go back down to the ground, but then the cold set in. I kept rotating which hand I held on to the tree with. When one hand got cold I'd pull it into my jacket sleeve and use the other hand to hold onto the tree. Once that one got cold, I'd trade hands again. After a while my legs and feet grew cold too. Pretty soon my whole body was shivering.

I could tell Melisa and Tyler were shaking too.

"We have to go back," Melisa said. Her voice quivered because of how cold she was.

"To the campsite?" Tyler asked.

"Are you nuts," I said, the best I could. My lips and jaw were too numb to really do what my brain was telling them to do. It made it hard to talk normal.

"You're slurring your words," Melisa said. "That's a sign of hypothermia. We're going to freeze to death without a fire. We need to get the backpack. The matches are in there."

# Chapter 16
# Stiff

Climbing down the tree made me realize how stiff my body was. It was hard to move my arms and legs. My fingers were worse. All my muscles felt like my lips and jaw. I couldn't get them to move the way I wanted. That's why I slipped on the way down the tree and fell to the ground.

Pain shot through my body, but I forced myself to stand, and follow Melisa and Tyler through the forest. We weren't sure where the campsite was, but thought we knew the way to the lake. We did find the lake and followed it back to the campsite.

Walking warmed me a little, but I still felt stiff and shivered. It made me clumsy. I stumbled over stones and roots that I normally wouldn't have.

We slowed as we neared the campsite. Nothing moved, but it was hard to tell if the bear was really gone. It was probably an expert at hiding.

I was going to propose that only one of us go into camp. After all, that's all it would take to get the backpack and leave. Then if the bear did attack, only one of us would be eaten. But the more I thought about it, the less realistic that idea seemed. If the person sent to get the backpack didn't get it, it's not like they'd be saving the lives of the other two people. Without the backpack, the other two would freeze. Bear or no bear, we needed fire. Might as well face the bear together.

We crept into camp. Katie and Melisa's shelter was demolished. Branches and sticks were thrown all over. The backpack was not far from where we had left it. It was torn open. Even though the bag was made of a strong durable material, it appeared that the bear had gotten into it as easily as the raccoons had gotten into Tyler's sock.

Melisa reached inside of the backpack. Then she turned it upside down. Only a few berries were left. Her fingers also looked stiff. "It's empty," she said, quickly pulling her hands back into her jacket's sleeves. "No matches."

"They haaa... haaave to bee-he here," I said. I went to the fire pit and held my hands close to the coals. I could only feel a little heat but wasn't sure if it was because the fire had grown that cool since we had been gone or if it was because my hands were too numb to feel the heat.

Tyler threw pine needles on the coals. "Maybe it accidently ate them when it was eating our berries," he said.

The pine needles smoked, then burst into flames. Tyler broke a piece of what used to be Katie and Melisa's shelter and tossed it on the fire too.

Melisa tried to yell, "Katie," but her voice was too weak to shout.

It was a relief to feel the warmth of the fire. I could finally start to bend my fingers again. "Let's warm ha-up. Then we-he-he can look for ha-her," I said, but knew we couldn't wait too long. Katie had to be freezing too.

# Chapter 17
# Search Party

Once warm enough to yell and move our fingers, we searched in the direction Katie had run.

We yelled, and walked, and yelled some more.

"Maybe it got her," Tyler said.

"We haven't found evidence of that," Melisa said. "We have to assume she's alive."

The way Melisa said "evidence" sent a different kind of shiver down my spine. Being hit by the bear's paw had shown me how powerful it was. It hadn't hit me hard. Just a swat, warning me to keep away. If it wanted to kill me it, could have in an instant. I couldn't imagine the damage it'd do to a person it really wanted to hurt. Now I was afraid to find Katie, or at least what was left of her.

"Katie," Melisa yelled.

The forest was silent and full of shadows. Finding her was going to be like finding a needle in a haystack.

Tyler stopped and held up his hand. "Wait," he said. "Listen."

I didn't know what I was listening for. I wanted it to be Katie, but instead I heard breathing again. At first, I thought it was the bear's deep breaths, but then I realized that whatever it was, it was breathing a lot faster than the bear had been. These were short, rapid breaths.

"This way," Tyler said.

The breathing grew louder and louder, until it sounded more like someone gasping for air, the way they do when they're crying. Then we found Katie. She was lying on the ground, curled in a ball, shivering, and sobbing.

Me and Tyler helped her up, but we couldn't get her to stand on her own. Her legs were too stiff.

"I wanwanna go hahaahome," Katie whined, before crying and shaking harder.

"Get her to the fire," Melisa said.

We practically carried her back to the lake and laid her in the shelter that was still standing. We threw wood on the fire, until there was a large blaze. Melisa put canteens next to the flames and made Katie drink from them once they warmed.

It took Katie a half hour to stop shivering and crying. Then she fell asleep. Melisa crawled into the shelter too. Me and Tyler laid as close to the fire as we could. Soon we were all sleeping.

# Chapter 18
# The Scream

When I woke up in the morning, Tyler and Melisa were already awake. Tyler was throwing one of the ropes into the air.

"What are you doing?" I asked.

"Hanging the backpack in a tree," he said.

Melisa looked up from her work, whittling the end of a stick to make a spear. "We should have done that in the first place," she said. "If we wouldn't have left food laying around camp the bear probably wouldn't have come. For now on, we'll make it a rule to tie up the backpack and throw all of our leftover fish far away from here."

Tyler coiled the rope up and tried to throw it again. I could tell which branch he was aiming for, but the rope didn't go high enough.

"It's too heavy," Tyler said, as he coiled the rope up again.

"Or not heavy enough," Melisa said, lifting a fist sized rock from the ground. "Help me tie this on."

While Tyler held the rock, Melisa wrapped the rope around it and tied several knots. When it was finished, Tyler held the rock like a baseball and threw it at the tree branch. The rock soared over the branch and fell to the ground on the other side, dragging the rope with it.

"Nice," Melisa said.

They pulled on the rope, hoisting the backpack in the air.

"We found the matches too." Melisa said. "They were laying..."

I turned to see why Melisa stopped talking. It was Katie. She wasn't in the shelter any more but standing by the lake.

We went to her, but Katie didn't look at us. She stared at the lake and the clouds beyond the mountain's rim.

Tyler leaned closer to her. "Katie?"

I don't really know what happened after that. I guess Katie just freaked out a little, because she took a deep breath and screamed at the top of her lungs. When she ran out of air, she took another breath, straitened her arms, leaned forward, and screamed some more.

Tyler backed away, but Melisa stepped forward and put her arms around Katie. As soon as Melisa started hugging her, the screaming stopped.

Katie's shoulders heaved, and she sobbed. "I hate this," Katie said. "I hate this."

I didn't know how to help. I'm not great at comforting people. I could have said something like, "It's okay" or "We'll be alright," but I didn't, because I was afraid it would be a lie. The truth was, we were stuck in the wilderness, a place where every living thing needs to fight to survive, even humans. It was just us, a bunch of kids vs. nature, and at that moment nature was really kicking our butts.

# Chapter 19
# Hanging in There

I hope you don't think Katie is psycho or anything, because she's not. People just react to fear, frustration, and near-death experiences differently. Don't be so sure that you wouldn't freak out if something like this happened to you. Katie pulled herself together about ten minutes later. She was still quiet after that, but given the circumstances, she handled things pretty well.

We were all a lot more motivated to look for cougars after that. Some days we walked around the lake, other days we followed the stream up the mountain, and more and more often we simply wondered through the forest.

I'll be honest, the forest was a creepy place after the bear came into camp. Sometimes I got the feeling that we were being watched, maybe stalked. It made it feel like we were living in a haunted house. You know, like something might jump out from behind a tree and scare us any second, except these monsters could actually eat us.

I wasn't the only one who felt this way. We carried our spears everywhere and made it a rule to stay close to at least one other person. I know that our wooden tipped spears wouldn't have helped much if a grizzly bear or mountain lion attacked, but it still made me feel a little safer.

Don't worry, I won't tell you all the details, because they're really boring. All we seemed to do was wake up in the morning and check our fish traps. Since we had more traps made, we usually had at least one or two fish to eat for the day, sometimes more, but sometimes none. Besides eating fish, looking for mountain lions, and making a shelter large enough for all of us to sleep inside, we didn't do a whole lot.

I was actually excited to go back to Mrs. Emmons class. Can you believe that? There we were, camping beside a lake, probably inside of one of the most beautiful mountain ranges in the world, and I wanted to go back to school. Trust me, I thought it was strange too, but the truth is, things get really boring in the forest once you've been there nearly two weeks.

After looking for mountain lions for such a long time, we were starting to wonder if any even lived on the mountain. At least I wondered if there were really some around. It's not like I actually talked to the others about this, because we were all scared enough the way it was. I'm pretty sure everyone else was wondering the same thing though. All I know for sure is that every evening, when I saw the first star appear in the sky, I made a wish that we would make it home alive.

# Chapter 20
# Wish Come True

Maybe we just got lucky, maybe it was a wish come true, or maybe it was just bound to happen sooner or later, but we finally found some cougar tracks. They were in the mud, beside the stream.

Katie crouched to look at them. "It's about time," she said.

Melisa put her hand on top of a paw print. "They're bigger than I was expecting."

"The question is, where is it?" I said, then turned to cough into my elbow, since I had a tickle in my throat.

"Let's spread out and see if we can find more," Melisa suggested.

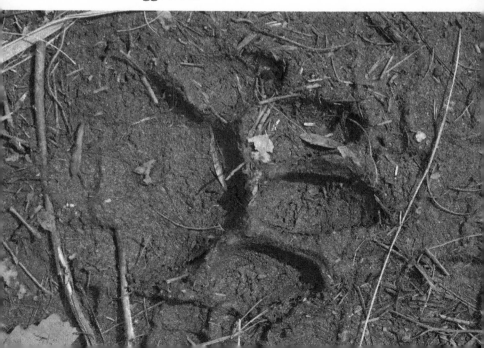

We looked all over the place for more tracks. You'd think I would have been excited about finding tracks, but I wasn't. I felt exhausted, like all my energy had drained away. Every step I took felt like a lot of work.

After a half hour of looking, we only found a couple more paw prints in the forest. That wasn't enough to follow where they went, so we decided to head back to camp.

"Are you alright," Tyler asked, since that tickle in my throat was making me cough again.

"Yea, I'm..." I had to cough a little more, "I'm fine."

"You look kind of pale," Melisa said.

"I'm just tired," I said. "I'll take a nap when we get back."

Since I felt so tired, it was a miserable hike back to camp. When we finally made it there, I crawled into the shelter and fell asleep.

# Chapter 21
# Fever

I tried to sit up, but a hand pushed me back. "Lay down," Melisa said.

My body felt sweaty and disgusting. I had that uncomfortable sensation of feeling like I was too hot and too cold at the same time.

"Did you guys cook the..." I coughed again, but this time it was a deep cough. Each time I took a breath my chest made a wheezing noise. "Did you guys eat already?" I asked.

"Last night," Tyler said.

"I slept all the way through the night?" I asked.

"And most of this morning too," Katie added.

Melisa picked up my canteen and handed it to me. "You should drink something."

I did take a few sips but started coughing some more.

"That sounds disgusting," Katie said.

Melisa put her hand on my forehead. "You're burning up," she said. She helped me screw the cap of my canteen back on, and then turned to Tyler and Katie. "He needs a doctor. You guys have to find a cougar."

# Chapter 22
# Breath

The others tell me that I had a fever for three days, and the wheezing from my lungs grew louder. Even after the fever went away I had a hard time breathing. My chest felt tight and I couldn't get a full breath of air. I took a bunch of little breaths and always felt winded.

Tyler and Katie left every morning to search for a mountain lion. Melisa didn't go with them. She stayed in the shelter, trying her best to care for me.

Even though I didn't have enough breath to talk, Melisa still talked to me. At first, she'd say things like, "Don't worry, you'll get better soon," and "It's going to be alright."

That wasn't very reassuring for me, especially since I felt worse each day. I don't know if you've ever had the feeling of not being able to breathe enough air, but it's really scary. I thought I might run out of oxygen any minute. That it wouldn't matter how fast I took my short, little breaths. Soon they wouldn't be enough to keep me alive.

Melisa started holding my hand and sometimes I heard her whispering prayers. She started to say things like "You have to get better" and "Don't give up" too.

Hearing her talk like that scared me. I remembered making a promise to tell her parents that she loved them during the last mission. I missed my family, even my little sister. I wanted to make Melisa promise me the same thing I had promised her, but it was impossible for me to talk.

I eventually started to cough up globs of green gunk. It was gross. At first, I just swallowed them, because I was too tired to sit up. Later, I managed to roll over and spit them outside the shelter. The others didn't like that, since they had to step over them to get in and out. Finally, Melisa brought me large pieces of tree bark to spit the globs onto, then carried them outside when they got full and threw them somewhere others wouldn't step on them or even have to see them.

# Chapter 23
# Frozen

One morning I actually felt a little better, but as soon as I opened my eyes, I figured I was going to die for sure. An inch of snow covered the ground outside the shelter. Even the tree branches were frosted white. The problem was, I wasn't just worried about me. I was worried about the others too. If winter was coming to the mountain, how would any of us be able to survive?

With the snow, came the cold. It got so cold that ice formed along the edges of the lake during the night. Tyler had to break the ice with rocks and sticks to get a fish that was in one of the traps. I don't know how he mustered up the will power to get into the water to catch it, but he did. For the first time in a while I was able to force myself to eat more than a few bites of fish.

"I hate to say it, but we might need to start using the deadfalls again," Melisa said.

"What do you mean," I asked.

Everyone was quiet for a moment.

"Our trap worked," Tyler finally said. "We caught a raccoon."

"Really," I asked.

"Yea, I was thinking about how the bear had come into our camp to eat the fish scraps. Then I had the idea to use some our fish as bait for the deadfall."

"And it worked?"

Tyler nodded.

"What's wrong?" I asked.

The others just looked at each other.

"Killing it made us sad," Melisa said. "It's not like eating a fish. It's cute and furry."

I thought back to our first mission, when the two raccoons came during the night. I could see where it might be hard to eat a raccoon. Their hands are shaped a lot like a person's and everything.

"It was kind of tough to chew," Katie added.

"We carried the rest of it a ways down the lake shore," Tyler said. "There's a cross shaped stick poking out of the ground where we buried it."

"We haven't used the deadfall since, but now that the lake is frozen we'll need to," Melisa said. "You guys should set it up today."

"Why don't you go out in the cold?" Katie asked.

"Someone needs to take care of Josh," Melisa said. She held one of my pieces of bark closer to Katie. "If you want to carry these outside be my guest."

Katie looked at the gunk laying on the bark, and then shook her head.

# Chapter 24
# Accident

"Just stop talking," Katie said, as her and Tyler walked back into camp. "I'm really mad at you right now."

"I said, 'I'm sorry.'"

Melisa raised her eyebrow before poking her head out the shelter. "Sorry for what?"

"He's sorry for killing us," Katie said. "We would all be back home right now if it wasn't for him."

Tyler's eyes were opened wider than normal and he seemed to be pleading with Katie. "It was an accident. I didn't mean to."

"What are you guys talking about?" Melisa asked.

"We finally saw a mountain lion, but Tyler scared it away."

"What do you mean, 'scared it away'?"

"Dummy here couldn't stay still long enough for me to take a picture. The phone was still off because of the low batteries. While it was turning on, he decided to get a better look at it."

"But I couldn't see it," Tyler said.

"Did you really have to see it," Katie shouted. "I told you not to move, and you did anyways." Katie put her hands on her hips. "He stepped on a stick, which made a snapping noise. By the time the phone was ready, it was gone."

"I didn't know it was going to be so spooked," Tyler said. "I was afraid it might come after us, not run away."

"Well that was probably our best chance of going home," Katie said. "Now we might be stuck here for good."

"But we can follow the tracks," Tyler said. He turned to Melisa to explain. "Now that it snowed the mountain lion left a good set of tracks to follow."

"We?" Katie repeated. "There is no 'we.' You're going to stay here with Josh tomorrow. You can't do anything right."

Tyler's eyes started to fill with tears, but Katie didn't stop her rant.

"You're the one who downloaded the app, you're the one who didn't read the terms and conditions, and now it's your fault that we don't have a picture of a mountain lion. All you do is screw things up for the rest of us."

"Hey, take it easy," I said. "It's not like he did it on purpose."

"And he said he's sorry," Melisa added.

"I don't care. It doesn't matter if he's sorry or not. We're stuck here because of him. Feeling sorry isn't going to save us."

# Chapter 25
# Gone

I'll admit, as bad as I felt for Tyler, I was upset with him too. It's hard not to be upset when you know that you were so close to being saved, and now it might not ever happen. Tyler was probably upset with himself too. He refused to talk the rest of the night, and sometimes I heard him sniffling.

When I woke up the next morning, Melisa was stepping back into the shelter.

"You guys, I think Tyler left," she said. "I don't see him out there, and it looks like his tracks are heading into the forest.

"He's probably going to set up his own campsite somewhere else," I said.

Melisa glared at Katie, "Can't blame him."

"You guys weren't there," Katie said. "The mountain lion was right in front of us and he scared it away. You'd be mad at him too."

"Trust me, I'm mad," I said. "But it doesn't mean that we have to hurt his feelings."

I'm gunna go look for him," Melisa said.

"Me too," I stood up for the first time since I had gotten sick. "I bet he'll camp close to the lake."

I followed Melisa out of the shelter. This was also my first time walking through the snow, which made me wish that I hadn't burned the hole in my shoe. Each time I took a step some of the

snowflakes fell onto my big toe. Soon the whole
front of my sock felt wet and cold.

"You guys," Katie called to us. "I think I know
where he is."

"Where?" Melisa asked.

"My phone is missing," Katie said. She held the
zipper pocket on her jacket open for us to see.
"He's trying to get the picture by himself."

# Chapter 26
# Red

We followed Tyler's tracks in the direction of yesterday's mountain lion sighting.

"I can't believe he stole it from me," Katie said. "He better not waste the battery or break it."

We walked fast, trying to catch up to him, even though the sun was melting the snow enough to make it slippery.

"That's the spot," Katie said. "It was sitting right there, next to the stump."

"He's gunna get himself hurt," Melisa said.

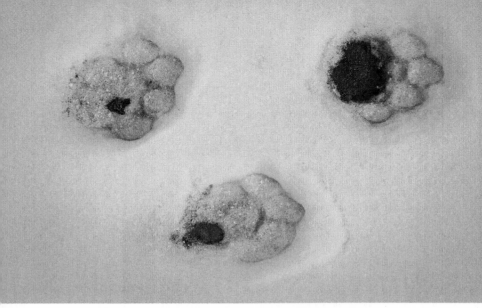

The mountain lion's trail wondered deep into the forest, and higher up the mountain. I could tell the cougar had strong legs, because in some places it had jumped over fallen trees. We usually had to climb over these logs or walk around them.

I glanced at the sun. "We have to hurry," I said. "The snow is melting. We can't track him if it's gone."

Melisa quickened her pace then stopped. She turned and covered her eyes.

"What is it?" I asked.

Melisa frowned, and her bottom lip quivered. She uncovered her eyes, but still didn't answer. She sniffed, then tears ran down her face.

I only had to take a few steps closer to Melisa to see what bothered her. Up ahead there was a large area of snow that wasn't white. The snow was stained red and there was a body lying in the center of it.

# Chapter 27
# Blood

"Maybe he's just hurt," I said, and rushed passed Melisa. "Come on, he needs help."

I slowed near the red area. I won't get into too many details, but everything looked a lot more gruesome than I anticipated. I could see chunks of flesh laying on the ground beside the body, but to my relief it wasn't Tyler's body. It was a deer, or at least what was left of a deer. Most of it had been eaten. Only its head and a couple legs were recognizable. The rest was mangled and missing.

"It's alright," I called. "It's not him."

Katie was already following me, but from a distance. Melisa hadn't come any closer and had her arms crossed over her stomach as if she was going to throw up.

"It's a deer," I yelled, trying to reassure her.

Finally, Melisa started walking again, but her steps were slower.

Katie threw her head back and shouted, "Tyler!"

She yelled again, and I joined her, but we didn't get a response.

"See, his tracks are right there," I told Melisa once she came close enough to see how Tyler's foot prints circled around the kill site and continued to follow the path the mountain lion took when it was done eating.

Now I realized we should've brought our spears with. I had been sick too long and forgot about them. Apparently, the others had gotten lazy and hadn't been carrying them around anymore either. Maybe that was a big mistake.

# Chapter 28
# What Just Happened?

We followed the tracks way up the mountain, where the forest thinned, and the ground was covered with more rocks than dirt.

Most of the snow melted, which not only made tracking hard, but made the rocks slippery. One spot was so slick, Melisa fell. It didn't take her long to stand up, but a few steps later she fell again. This time I think she landed harder, because she paused a while before trying to stand, like she was waiting a few moments for the pain to go away.

Since I was right behind her, I held out my hand to help her. "Are you alright?" I asked.

She took my hand and pulled herself up.

"Thanks," she said.

Okay, now I don't really know how to explain this. I'm not sure if it's the way she said "thanks," or if it was the way she looked at me after and smiled, but I suddenly got that exciting, scary, weak feeling that happened when I held Katie's hand in the desert.

At first, I thought maybe that's just the way I get when I hold a girl's hand. The thing is, I stood there and waited by that slippery spot, so I could help Katie cross it too, but this time when I held her hand I didn't get that feeling. It just felt like I was holding someone's hand.

After that, I stopped paying attention to Tyler's tracks. I just followed the girls up the mountain. I was too busy thinking and trying to understand what just happened.

It took me a while, but I finally thought I figured it out. Maybe that feeling isn't as strong when I hold two people's hands right in a row, like the way a loud noise makes you jump the first time you hear it, but not a second time because by then you're expecting it to be loud.

# Chapter 29
# Cave

Katie stopped and pointed. "There he is," she said.

Not far ahead, Tyler was crouching by a rock and looking away from us.

"Hey, Tyler," I called.

I could tell he heard me, because he turned to look at us. He didn't glance long though.

We walked closer to him.

"What's he doing?" Katie asked.

"Tyler," Melisa yelled.

Tyler turned again. He put a finger to his lips and was holding the cell phone in the same hand.

"I think he sees it," Katie said.

"Then why doesn't he take a picture?" Melisa asked.

"What are you doing?" I asked, as we came closer.

"I was here before the snow melted," Tyler said. "Its tracks go in and out of that cave."

I looked at the cave entrance. I don't know if I would call it a cave, but there was a gap between two boulders that were leaning together. It did look like a good place for a mountain lion den.

"Give me my phone back," Katie said, "and if you ever think about stealing it again..."

Katie stopped talking once Tyler turned around to hand the phone back. The left side of his face looked swollen, scratched, and bruised.

"What happened?" Melisa asked.

Tyler waited for Katie to take the phone from his hand. Then he turned to watch the den's entrance again.

"Was it the cougar?"

Tyler shook his head.

"What happened then?" Melisa asked.

Tyler took a deep breath. The breath was shaky. He bit his bottom lip to keep from frowning. "I slipped on the rocks," he said quietly, as if he was ashamed to say it.

I glanced at Katie, but she was staring at the ground.

"Does your head hurt?" Melisa asked. "You could have a concussion."

Tyler shook his head. "My arm hurts. I think it might be broken."

"Let's take a look," Melisa said.

Tyler unzipped his jacket with one hand. I could tell that he was trying hard to keep the other arm as still as possible, so I helped him take the jacket off. I tried to be gentle, but his face still grimaced when we slide the sleeve off his bad arm.

"Oh my gosh," Katie said.

Tyler's arm wasn't strait like an arm is supposed to be. It was bent, and you could see exactly where the broken bone was because his skin bulged under the pressure of it being out of place and a gross bruise had formed around it.

Just to warn you, I have a picture of the way his arm looked on the next page, so if you don't want to see something nasty like that just skip to page 91 instead.

Last warning…

See, I told you it's nasty.

Feel free to barf now. I almost did.

# Chapter 30
# Cave

"Well it's definitely broken," I said.

Tyler's eyes were wide, and his face turned pale. It was like he was getting sick, just from looking at his injury.

"You're going to need a splint," Melisa said. "It'll help keep it still."

"Shouldn't the bone be set back in place first?" Katie asked.

"Yea, but," Melissa hesitated. She stared at the bulge on his arm a while longer. "We can't. We might make it worse," she decided. "Besides I don't think I could do it." Then she looked at me. "Unless Josh, If you think..."

She didn't even finish that thought because I quickly shook my head and backed up a few steps. "No way," I said. "Let's just focus on getting that picture."

We waited while Melisa gathered supplies for a splint. She pulled branches off the few trees that were growing on this part of the mountain.

"I'm sorry for saying those things to you yesterday," Katie said. "I didn't mean them."

Tyler shook his head. "No, you were right. You guys really would be better off if I wasn't here."

"That's not true," Katie said. "I was just upset when I said that."

"But I do mess everything up," Tyler said. "I thought I could get a picture of the cougar and prove that I wasn't a screw up, but all I did was prove that I am."

"Anyone could have slipped," I said. "Melisa fell on our way up too."

Tyler seemed to sit up a little straighter after he heard this. "Really?"

"Yea," Katie said. "Sometimes accidents happen."

"I've just never been a part of a team like this before," Tyler said. "I mean, I know Mrs. Emmons picked our groups that day, but... I don't know. I just wish I could do a better job of helping everyone out."

I thought about how Tyler always sat by himself during lunch at school. He didn't really have friends that he hung out with. Being around each other on the missions probably felt like a bigger deal for him than it did for the rest of us.

"You're really brave," Katie said. "I wouldn't have had the guts to track a mountain lion by myself. Especially after seeing what it did to that deer."

"Yea, you put yourself in danger so that we could all go back home," I said. "Maybe you didn't get the picture, but at least you found where the cougar lives."

"But that's not really what team members do," Katie said. "I know I said that I wanted you to stay in camp today with Josh, but the truth is, we should always be working as a team. Next time we'll go together."

Melisa returned, carrying some sticks. "These were the straightest ones I could find," she said. "Now we just need something to tie them with."

I looked down at my jacket and saw the string that's used to tighten the hood. Since we didn't bring the backpack, which had the ropes in it, I pulled the string out of my jacket.

"Here," I said. "Try this."

Melisa took the string from me. "Perfect, but I'm going to need the others too."

We pulled the strings out of all the jackets. Melisa used two of them to make the splint. Then she used the other two to make a sling, to help hold Tyler's arm by his side.

# Chapter 30
# Evening

I don't think it's even in there, "Katie said.

The sun was lowering closer to the mountaintops, and the air was starting to chill.

"Well, if we don't see anything soon we should go back to camp," Melisa said.

"You have the matches. Don't you?" I asked.

Melisa nodded. She always carried some in her pocket, since the night the bear came into camp.

"Yea, but I'm not camping in front of a mountain lion den. We can come back tomorrow."

"But what if it doesn't come back?" Tyler asked. "Maybe it knows we're waiting for it and once it leaves it'll find somewhere else to live."

Melisa crossed her arms and looked down at the lake. I could tell she was nervous.

"Maybe we should try getting it to come out," I said. "Or at least find out of its actually in there."

"And how do you plan to do that?" Melisa asked.

I wanted to say that we could throw rocks inside the den and see if it would growl at us or something, but throwing rocks just brought back bad memories of the moose mission.

"I don't know. Maybe we could light a torch," I suggested. "Then we could at least look in the den long enough to take a picture."

"and what if it attacks?" Melisa asked.

"If it's scared and waiting for us to leave, maybe it won't attack," I said. "Besides, as long as someone takes a picture of it, we will only need to worry about that for a minute. Then the app should take us home."

Nobody said anything for a while. We looked at the den and thought about our options.

"I say we give it a try," Katie said. "We've almost been here a month, and now that the lake is frozen we won't have any more fish to eat. I just want to go home, even if it does mean a minute with a mountain lion."

It took a long time to tie grass and pine needles to the end of some sticks. They looked like nice torches to me, until Melisa suggested that we test one before going to the den. The torch lit fine, but it didn't burn very long. As soon as the grass that was holding it all together burned, the rest of the grass and pine needles fell off the stick too.

Melisa put her hands on her hips. "Well that's not going to work."

"Just forget the torches," Katie said, "The needles burned the best anyways. Let's light a whole branch on fire."

"That still won't last very long." Melisa said.

"Long enough to get a picture," Katie insisted.

"Let's do it," I said, and left to find a dead pine branch that had a lot of dried needles on it.

I hadn't gone far when something caught my eye. It was a mountain lion, crouching by some rocks, and it was looking right at me.

# Chapter 32
# Creepy Eyes

As soon as I made eye contact with the cougar it stood, not all the way, but partway, the way cats do when they're stalking something. It took a couple steps in my direction.

I stepped back, closer to the others, always keeping my eyes on the cat. "You guys," I called.

"What?" Melisa called back.

They didn't see it, but I was in too much shock to explain. It stayed low to the ground and only took a step forward when I took a step back.

"Take a picture," Melisa screamed, once she realized what was happening.

"It's turning on," Katie said.

I walked faster, still keeping my eyes on the cougar. I stumbled. The cougar bounded toward me. I caught myself from falling with my hand and stood quickly. I was getting ready for the attack, which seemed to be moments away. Then I heard Tyler yelling from behind me.

"HHHAaaaaaaaa."

The sound of running feet came closer to me. Tyler appeared by my side.

The cougar slowed. It was cautious now that there were two of us. It walked within pouncing distance, then stopped to open its mouth and hiss, giving us a fantastic view of its fangs.

"Got it," Katie yelled.

"Keep yelling," Melisa shouted.

I could hear more footsteps rushing closer.

Me and Tyler yelled and screamed at the mountain lion. It hissed, circled for a better position, then lowered its body to jump.

"Go on. Get out of here," Melisa yelled. She was beside us now.

Katie was not far behind. I could hear the app say, "Returning home in 45 seconds."

The mountain lion stood again. It even took a step back, yet it's eyes never left me.

"Doo Daa."

"You guys. The battery is practically gone," Katie said. she closed the 'low battery' warning box that appeared on the screen.

"Returning home in 30 seconds..."

The cougar stared at us, the creepy way cats do, like it was more intelligent than us and was developing a plan to make us its prey.

Melisa took off her jacket and waved it around.
The mountain lion seemed annoyed by the
flapping. It took a couple steps back.

"Returning home in..."

"Doo Daa."

"Come on, you can do it," Katie said to the
phone.

I took my jacket off too and waved it through
the air as hard as I could. All our yelling and jacket
waving finally made the mountain lion turn and
trot further away. It didn't go very far before it
stopped and looked over its shoulder again.

"Returning home in 5... 4... 3... 2... 1... Doo Daa..."

Nothing happened.

Alright, I guess a better way to describe it is NOTHING HAPPENED!

I stopped waving my jacket and turned in time to see Katie clear the low battery warning box again. As soon as she touched the screen, it glowed brighter and brighter. Then the pulse of light appeared.

# Chapter 33
# Brave

When my eyes opened again, we were in Mrs. Emmons' room. The first person I saw was Tyler. He held his arm, turning his wrist back and forth. The lump from his broken bone was gone.

Melisa smiled at me from across the room and I got that weird feeling again.

"Doo... Daa..."

The class looked in Katie's direction. Mrs. Emmons' eyes darted back and forth.

Katie sat still and glanced around too, pretending that she didn't know where the noise came from. Katie focused on her work again. The rest of the class did the same. Even Mrs. Emmons lost interest. Katie casually reached into her pocket, probably turning off the phone so it wouldn't make more sounds.

I looked in Melisa's direction one more time, but she was working again too. I was about to do the same, when I noticed John was ripping more pieces from his paper and crumpling them into little balls.

That's when I remembered Tyler, his binder, and how he had run to my side when the mountain lion was attacking. He risked his life for me, even though I had been too chicken to stick up for him any of the thousand times John Marten had picked on him.

Suddenly, it seemed strange that Tyler always ate lunch by himself. For someone who didn't have any friends, he was sure good at being one.

John tossed the paper balls at Tyler.

I stood up. "Knock it off jerk."

Alright, I didn't really call him a jerk, but I did tell him to "knock it off," and grabbed Tyler's binder from under John's papers. "Hey Tyler, is this yours?" I asked.

Tyler merely nodded. He seemed too scared to say anything, or maybe too surprised.

"What a party pooper," John said and tossed the rest of his paper balls at me.

# Chapter 34
# An Outcast

John had a special interest in picking on me the rest of the morning. In math class, he went to sharpen his pencil. As he walked by my desk he knocked over my books with his elbow. When he walked back, he made sure his elbow bumped into the back of my head too.

For the first time since elementary school started, I didn't sit by Mark, John or any of the other kids I usually ate lunch with. I had been picked on enough for one day. Instead I went to Tyler's end of the table and sat down. I hoped Mark would join me, but he didn't.

"You know what? I've been thinking," Tyler said. He moved his playing cards to the side, so I had more room to eat. "Maybe since we're all going to be in different places this weekend, the app won't be able to send us anywhere."

John pretended to sneeze, but covered his mouth and said, "Losers," at the same time.

People laughed at his end of the table.

"I sure hope so," I told Tyler, and really meant it too. All I wanted was a few days off—No missions, no bullies, no worries.

# 👍 Next in the Series

# About Cougars

## Quick Facts
Length: 7-8 ft. from nose to tail.
Weight:  Can be over 200 pounds.
Running Speed: Up to 50 mph.
Jump: Can leap 15 ft. high and 40 ft across.
Diet: Meat (deer, elk, raccoons, rabbits, mice)

## How Dangerous Are They?
Cougars do attack and kill people, but these are extremely rare occurrences. They prefer to avoid humans and are very good at it. Tracks and the remains of prey animals are usually the only signs of their presence.

## What if You Do See a Cougar?
Everyone seems to agree that you should stay calm and give it space. Also, if you're with other people, stay close together. Normally cougars will leave you alone if you leave them alone.

Beyond this advice, most experts say not to run. This might entice the cat to chase you. Never turn your back to a cougar because they prefer to attack prey from behind and bite the back of their necks. Instead, back away, try to act big and strong, and fight back if it does attack.

On the other hand, a few experts disagree with this second paragraph. They say running away is the best option. It distances you from the cat and proves you're strong and healthy, which might discourage an attack. So, use your best judgement and know that I won't blame you if you do decide to run.

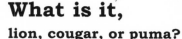

# What is it,
## lion, cougar, or puma?

**Cougar Range**

Mountain lions have at least 40 different names. Why so many for one animal? Well, mountain lions don't just live in mountains. They live in deserts, jungles, and swamps too. Their range covers a lot of western North America and most of South America.

As a result, people from many cultures are exposed to cougars and have named them different things. Some names include mountain lion, cougar, panther, puma, cat of god, catamount, devil cat, silver lion, ghost cat, and my personal favorite, swamp screamer.

## Kittens

Mountain lions are born with spots and bright blue eyes. As they grow the spots disappear and their eyes turn yellow. Did I mention they're super cute? Head to karlsteam.com if you want to learn more about mountain lions or to watch a video about mountain lion kittens.

# Bear Safety

Preventing contact with a bear is the best way to stay safe. Leaving food out can attract bears and cause problems. Making lots of noise while hiking can give bears a chance to hear you coming and give them time to move out of your way.

## Black Bears vs. Brown Bears

Safety tips differ depending on which species you're dealing with. For instance, experts recommend playing dead if a brown bear attacks, because resisting or fleeing often aggravates them more, but with black bears they encourage people to try escaping and to fight back.

One recommendation that does stay the same is not to leave food out that could attract them to you or where they can get to it.

# Eating Acorns

Native Americans ate acorns for thousands of years, often putting them in soups or grinding them into flower for breads. Tannic acids make raw acorns taste bitter, but boiling water can leach a lot of these acids away. This reduces the bitterness and exposes their sweet, nutty flavors instead.

Don't try eating acorns without a trusted adult to help. Some species of oaks have more tannins than others. If selected or prepared improperly you could get sick. Too much tannins can irritate your digestive system and acorns sometimes have worms growing inside of them.

# Would You Survive the Wild?

## Staying Warm

Weather can be unpredictable in the mountains, so always bring extra layers of clothing when hiking or camping there. Knowing how to start a fire and find shelter in an emergency is important too. Even a crude shelter made of branches can help block wind and rain.

## Broken Bones and Other Injuries

It's often a good idea to make a splint for broken bones and sprained joints. Sticks or other solid objects can help immobilize the area and prevent further injury. If there are open wounds, try to keep them clean and cover with a cloth.

## Deadfalls and Fish Traps

There are many kinds of deadfalls and fish traps and can be very effective at catching game, but please don't make either without the help of an adult. They're also illegal to use in most places and potentially harmful to animals, so maybe wait for a true emergency before trying to make one.

Made in the USA
Middletown, DE
18 March 2020